About the Author

Katherine Ruskey has been writing stories since she was seven years old. Her very first story was "published" in the basement of her parent's house, where she and her sister had their very own teacher's chalkboard. Katie loves being outdoors, taking road trips to the beach, and snuggling her yellow lab, Cooper.

THE A B "SEAS"
OF OCEAN CITY,
MARYLAND

Katherine Ruskey

AUSTIN MACAULEY PUBLISHERS™

LONDON * CAMBRIDGE * NEW YORK * SHARJAH

Copyright © Katherine Ruskey (2018)

Ordering Information:
Quantity sales: special discounts are available on quantity purchases by corporations, associations, and others. For details, contact the publisher
at the address below.

Katherine Ruskey
The A B "Seas" of Ocean City, Maryland

ISBN 9781641820738 (Paperback)
ISBN 9781641820714 (Hardback)
ISBN 9781641820721 (E-Book)

The main category of the book — JUVENILE NONFICTION / Travel
www.austinmacauley.com/us

First Published (2018)
Austin Macauley Publishers™ LLC
40 Wall Street, 28th Floor
New York, NY 10005
USA

mail-usa@austinmacauley.com
+1 (646) 5125767

Dedication

To the beaches, boardwalk, and sunsets - Thanks for the memories.

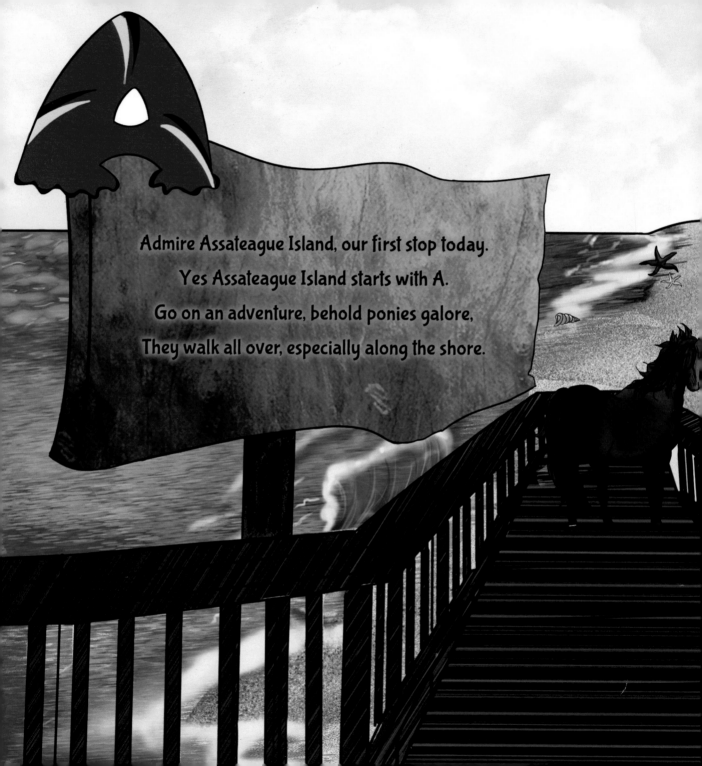

Admire Assateague Island, our first stop today.

Yes Assateague Island starts with A.

Go on an adventure, behold ponies galore,

They walk all over, especially along the shore.

Boogie board and body surf down to the beach,

Always stay close so your feet will reach,

The boardwalk is always a great place to relax,

Play ball, ride bikes, or just laugh, laugh, laugh.

Clamor to Candy Kitchen, the best stop for some sweets,
Caramel apples, chocolate fudge, and other sugary treats,
Come to the bayside and give me your hand,
We'll dig—*clickitty, clattity, clump*—clams.

Get off to the Gallery for gorgeous art,
Or go over the bridge and get on the go—carts,
Take a gander at a gander out on the bay,
Or gaze at the ocean and watch fishing boats sway.

Have a scare in the house that haunts the Inlet,

Howls and screams are heard from guests who visit,

Or pick up a souvenir, maybe a hermit crab,

Handle him gentle so he won't pinch and get mad.

Jiggle for jellyfish, not a fish you can eat,

Jellies float and sting but never are mean,

Jump towards the rides at Jolly Roger for a swing,

You can slide, glide, or fly, just about anything.

Catch a wave down to 5th Street for some flying fun, The Kite
Loft is there, kites are always catching some sun,
Kaboodles of kids are carrying newly bought kites,
They can't wait until the wind is blowing just right.

Listen to the lifeguards, they're there for your safety,
They make sure that you are having fun safely,
Their whistles are loud so you can hear,
When they call you from the ocean making sure you are near.

Make wake in a marina, a place to dock boats,

Secure the knots tight so away they don't float,

Blue marlins and white are overflowing the sea,

Fishing tournaments are notorious, charter captains agree.

Navigate towards the Route 50 Bridge,

There you can toss out a rod and "catch you some fish,"

Nab a night crawler, attach to the end of your line,

Throw out a cast, it's only a matter of time.

Into the early misty morning, quiet you will hear,

The only sound is the waves crashing close to the pier,

Tranquil and calm the mornings await,

Kids with their sand buckets, quick to start their play.

Roaring rip currents should be taken with caution,
When rowing or swimming in the rolling ocean,
At night run to Trimper's Rides near the boardwalk's end,
Carousels, Ferris wheels, and rollercoasters roll and bend.

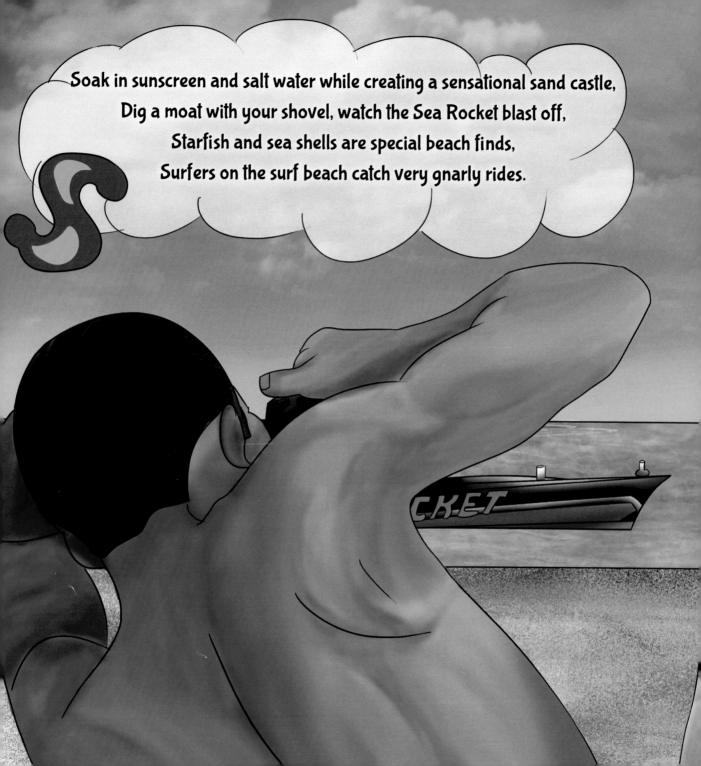

Hear the ting—a—ling—ling of the Telescope workers,
Take a break from your swimming and pose for a picture,
Make a muscle, hug your sister, and try your best goofy face,
Take off to the boardwalk for a train ride you race.

Vacation, oh vacation, when people can rest,
Ocean City is terrific for this, some even say the best,
Visitors are in awe of this great vacation spot,
All are welcome, the younger, the older, and especially tots.

Wave in Worcester County, home to Ocean City,
This county is far from being itty bitty,
Wet suits are worn to keep warm in the water,
But usually in winter; it's too hot in the summer.

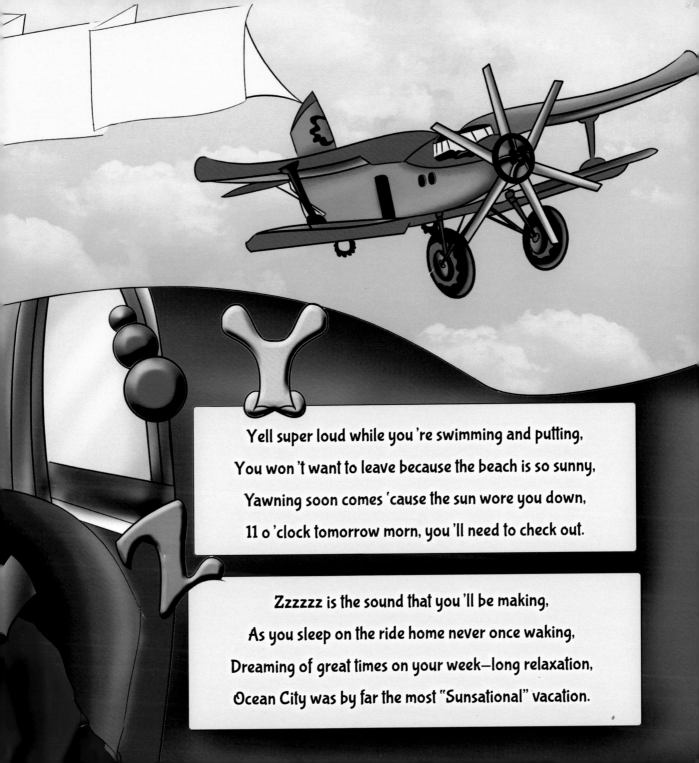

Yell super loud while you're swimming and putting,

You won't want to leave because the beach is so sunny,

Yawning soon comes 'cause the sun wore you down,

11 o'clock tomorrow morn, you'll need to check out.

Zzzzzz is the sound that you'll be making,

As you sleep on the ride home never once waking,

Dreaming of great times on your week–long relaxation,

Ocean City was by far the most "Sunsational" vacation.